SLUMBERFAIRY FALLS

I wish, I wish
With all my heart
To fly with dragons
In a land apart.

By Jennifer Liberts Weinberg
Illustrated by The Thompson Brothers
Based on the characters by Ron Rodecker

Visit Dragon Tales on the Web at www.dragontales.com
Watch us on PBS!

It was very late at night in Dragon Land when Ord was awakened by a bad dream.

"A purple goo cloud was following me all around," Ord told his dragon bear. "Sticky, icky goo was everywhere!"

With that, Ord hid under the covers and waited for morning to come.

The next day, in the middle of class, Cassie heard a loud snore and turned around.

"Ord! Wake up!" she whispered, shaking the big dragon gently.

Ord yawned and rubbed his eyes. "I'm *soooo* sleepy," he said. "I keep having bad dreams at night and can't fall back to sleep!"

"Oh, Ord," said Cassie, "I wish I could chase away those bad dreams for you."

That night, Ord brushed his teeth and gave his mom a hug and a kiss before he climbed into bed.

He sat up long after bedtime, afraid to go to sleep. Then he had a bright idea. "I can't have a nightmare if I don't go to sleep," he said. "Maybe I can read all night long!"

But as he read, Ord's eyelids got heavier and heavier. Before long, he was fast asleep.

Tucked under his cozy quilt, Ord began to dream that he had showed up at school in pink polka-dot pajamas! He was so embarrassed!

"Oh, my!" said Ord as he woke with a start.

At that moment, Ord saw three sparkling little fairies swoop in through the window.

"Am I still dreaming?" he wondered aloud to his dragon bear.

Then, with a little *poof,* the sparkly creatures flew out of the bedroom window, leaving a trail of glitter behind. As the creatures passed him, Ord felt a breeze tickle his ear and knew for sure that he was awake. But he soon drifted off to sleep again, and when he did, he dreamed happy dreams for the rest of the night.

"Morning, Ord!" said Max and Emmy, peeking in the door of Ord's room early the next morning.

"Emmy! Max! You're here! I'm so glad to see you," shouted Ord. The big dragon jumped out of bed to give his friends a huge hug.

"Cassie told us you were having bad dreams," said Emmy.
"Did you have one last night?" asked Max.
Ord told them about the sparkly fairies he'd seen. He pointed to the fading sparkly trail they'd left behind. "After they came, I had only good dreams," he said.

Soon Cassie, Zak, and Wheezie arrived at Ord's house to see if they could help, too.

"Look," said Zak. "There's sparkly dust in Ord's room!"

"Oh! That must be from the slumberfairies!" Wheezie exclaimed. "They're tiny fairies that live by Slumberfairy Falls. They chase away bad dreams."

"I want a slumberfairy in my room all the time!" Ord declared. "How do I find one?"

"Let's follow their slumberdust trail to Slumberfairy Falls," Cassie suggested.

On the way to Slumberfairy Falls, Zak and Wheezie played a cheerful tune on their scales to give their friends a rhythm to walk to.

"That gives me an idea," said Wheezie. "Music helps *me* dream happy dreams. I'll give you my tambourine to play before bedtime, Ord."

"And I'll teach you a lullaby to hum!" Zak offered.

"Maybe you could think happy thoughts before you go to sleep," suggested Emmy.

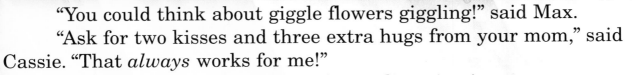

"You could think about giggle flowers giggling!" said Max.

"Ask for two kisses and three extra hugs from your mom," said Cassie. "That *always* works for me!"

No one noticed some slumberfairies listening in.

All of a sudden the slumberdust trail ended at a gushing, glittering waterfall.

"Look!" cried Ord. "The water sparkles!"

"This must be Slumberfairy Falls!" said Cassie.

And just then, a friendly slumberfairy appeared and greeted the friends with a warm hello.

Ord told the slumberfairy all about his bad dreams. "You helped me get rid of my bad dream last night. Would you come live with me so I'll never have a bad dream again?" Ord asked.

"We can't be with you all the time, Ord," said the slumberfairy. "There are other dragons who need our help, too."

"So what will I do?" Ord asked with a sigh.

"You already know how to chase bad dreams away on your own," said the slumberfairy. "Just remember the good ideas your friends shared with you."

"You're right!" Ord cried. "I *can* do it all by myself!"

That night, Ord woke again from a bad dream. But this time he was determined—he would chase it away on his own! So he called to his mom and asked for two kisses and three extra hugs. Then he shook Wheezie's tambourine, hummed a lullaby, and thought about happy things like dragonberry cupcakes and somersaults.

"Good night, li'l Dragon Bear," Ord said happily as his eyes closed. Soon he was fast asleep again.

And all night long, snuggled in his cozy bed, the big blue dragon dreamed lots of sweet, happy dreams.